A NOTE TO PARENTS

When your children are ready to "step into reading," giving them the right books—and lots of them—is as crucial as giving them the right food to eat. **Step into Reading Books** present exciting stories and information reinforced with lively, colorful illustrations that make learning to read fun, satisfying, and worthwhile. They are priced so that acquiring an entire library of them is affordable. And they are beginning readers with an important difference—they're written on four levels.

    Step 1 Books, with their very large type and extremely simple vocabulary, have been created for the very youngest readers. **Step 2 Books** are both longer and slightly more difficult. **Step 3 Books,** written to mid-second-grade reading levels, are for the child who has acquired even greater reading skills. **Step 4 Books** offer exciting nonfiction for the increasingly proficient reader.

    Children develop at different ages. **Step into Reading Books,** with their four levels of reading, are designed to help children become good—and interested—readers *faster*. The grade levels assigned to the four steps—preschool through grade 1 for Step 1, grades 1 through 3 for Step 2, grades 2 and 3 for Step 3, and grades 2 through 4 for Step 4—are intended only as guides. Some children move through all four steps very rapidly; others climb the steps over a period of several years. These books will help your child "step into reading" in style!

For Jane O'Connor
—C.S.

Library of Congress Cataloging-in-Publication Data
Siracusa, Catherine. No mail for Mitchell. (Step into reading. A step 1 book) SUMMARY: Mitchell the mailman loves delivering mail to all the animals on his postal route, but he does not receive any mail himself until sickness forces him to leave the route for a day. [1. Postal service—Letter carriers—Fiction. 2. Animals—Fiction. 3. Sick—Fiction] I. Title. II. Series: Step into reading. Step 1 book. PZ7.S6215No 1990 [E] 89-70010 ISBN 0-679-80476-5 ISBN 0-679-90476-X (lib. bdg.)

Manufactured in the United States of America   13   14   15   16   17   18   19   20

STEP INTO READING is a trademark of Random House, Inc.

Step into Reading

No Mail
for
Mitchell

By Catherine Siracusa

A Step 1 Book

Random House 🏠 New York

Mitchell is a mailman.
Every day he delivers
a big sack of mail.

He brings a letter
up to Mr. Owl.

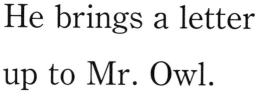

He carries a package
down to Mrs. Groundhog.

Mitchell brings
a magazine
to Mrs. Mouse.

And a box of books
to the Beaver family.

But when he comes home,
there is no mail
for Mitchell.

"Everyone gets mail but me,"
says Mitchell.

Then Mitchell has an idea.

He writes:

Mitchell goes outside
to mail the letter
to himself.

But it is a windy
and rainy night.
The wind blows
his letter away!

Mitchell goes back home.

He is very sad.

"I will never get any mail."

When he gets inside,

the phone is ringing.

It is his boss, Mr. Pig.

"I know it is late,"

he says.

"But I have a special package

for Bobby Beaver.

Will you deliver it tonight?"

Mitchell hurries

to the post office.

"I can always count on you!"

Mr. Pig tells him.

Then he gives Mitchell

the package.

Mitchell goes out again
into the rain.
The wind blows his umbrella
inside out.

Splash! He steps
in a big puddle.

"I am all wet," says Mitchell.
"But the mail
    must go through."

At last he sees
the Beavers' house.
"Special delivery!"
shouts Mitchell.

Mr. Beaver answers the door.

"We are so glad to see you!

You have Bobby's present

from Grandma Beaver.

Please come inside."

Mitchell tries to dry off.
Bobby asks,
"Will you have
some birthday cake?"

But Mitchell says,

"No, thank you.

It is late.

I have to get home.

Happy Birthday, Bobby!"

Mitchell goes back
to his house.
He takes off
his wet clothes.
He puts on his dry pajamas.
"I am tired," says Mitchell.
"But I got the job done."

The next morning
Mitchell wakes up
with a bad cold.

He calls the post office.
Mr. Pig says to
take a few days off.
He will deliver the mail
for Mitchell.

For two days

Mitchell stays in bed.

He drinks tea with honey.

He reads books.

He watches TV.

But he misses his job.

The next morning
the doorbell rings.
It is Mr. Pig.
He hands Mitchell
a big bag of mail.
"Mail for me?"
"Yes! Mail for you!"
says Mr. Pig.

Mitchell opens a letter.

It says:

DEAR MITCHELL,
GET WELL SOON!
SINCERELY,
MR. OWL

And a postcard says:

Another letter says:

Then Mitchell opens
a large card.
"It is a picture of me!"
he says.

Inside, the card says:

"You are a good mailman,
Mitchell," says Mr. Pig.

Mitchell smiles.

"It is nice to be a mailman,"
he says.

"And it is nice to get mail."